APPLEY DAPPLY'S
NURSERY RHYMES

APPLEY DAPPLY'S
NURSERY RHYMES

BY

BEATRIX POTTER

Author of
" *The Tale of Peter Rabbit,*" *etc.*

FREDERICK WARNE

*Frederick Warne has a continuing commitment to reproduce
Beatrix Potter's exquisite watercolours to the highest possible standard.
In 1993 and 1994, taking advantage of the latest advances in printing
technology and expertise, entirely new film was made from her original
book illustrations. The drawings are now reproduced with a quality
and a degree of authenticity never before attainable in print.*

FREDERICK WARNE

Published by the Penguin Group
27 Wrights Lane, London W8 5TZ, England
Penguin Books USA Inc., 375 Hudson Street, New York, N.Y . 10014, USA
Penguin Books Australia Ltd, Ringwood, Victoria, Australia
Penguin Books Canada Ltd, 10 Alcorn Avenue, Toronto, Ontario, Canada M4V 3B2
Penguin Books (N.Z.) Ltd, 182-190 Wairau Road, Auckland 10, New Zealand

Penguin Books Ltd, Registered Offices: Harmondsworth, Middlesex, England

First published 1917 by Frederick Warne
This edition with new reproductions of Beatrix Potter's book
illustrations first published 1995

Colour reproduction by
Saxon Photolitho Ltd, Norwich
Printed and bound in Great Britain by
William Clowes Limited, Beccles and London

APPLEY DAPPLY, a little
brown mouse,
Goes to the cupboard in somebody's house.

IN somebody's cupboard
    There's everything nice,
Cake, cheese, jam, biscuits,
    —All charming for mice !

APPLEY DAPPLY has little
sharp eyes,
And Appley Dapply is *so* fond
of pies !

NOW who is this knocking
    at Cottontail's door ?
Tap tappit !   Tap tappit !
    She's heard it before ?

ND when she peeps out
there is nobody there,
But a present of carrots
put down on the stair.

HARK ! I hear it again !
Tap, tap, tappit ! Tap
tappit !
Why—I really believe it's a
little black rabbit !

OLD Mr. Pricklepin
has never a cushion to
stick his pins in,
His nose is black and his
beard is gray,
And he lives in an ash stump
over the way.

YOU know the old woman
who lived in a shoe?
And had so many children
She didn't know what to
do?

I THINK if she lived in
  a little shoe-house—
That little old woman was
  surely a mouse !

DIGGORY DIGGORY
DELVET !
A little old man in black
velvet ;
He digs and he delves—
You can see for yourselves
The mounds dug by Diggory
Delvet.

GRAVY and potatoes
    In a good brown pot—
Put them in the oven,
    and serve them very hot !

THERE once was an amiable
    guinea-pig,
Who brushed back his hair like
    a periwig—

H^E wore a sweet tie,
As blue as the sky—

AND his whiskers and
buttons
Were very big.

The "PETER RABBIT" BOOKS
by BEATRIX POTTER

PETER RABBIT · SQUIRREL NUTKIN
TAILOR OF GLOUCESTER · BENJAMIN BUNNY
TWO BAD MICE · MRS. TIGGY - WINKLE
MR. JEREMY FISHER · TOM KITTEN
JEMIMA PUDDLE-DUCK · THE FLOPSY BUNNIES
MRS. TITTLEMOUSE · TIMMY TIPTOES
JOHNNY TOWN-MOUSE · MR. TOD
PIGLING BLAND · SAMUEL WHISKERS
THE PIE & THE PATTY-PAN · GINGER & PICKLES
LITTLE PIG ROBINSON

A FIERCE BAD RABBIT   MISS MOPPET
APPLEY DAPPLY'S   CECILY PARSLEY'S
NURSERY RHYMES   NURSERY RHYMES
     PETER RABBIT'S   TOM KITTEN'S
     PAINTING BOOK   PAINTING BOOK